AFTER

DARK

AFTER DARK

Teryl Euvremer

Crown Publishers, Inc.
New York

Published by Crown Publishers, Inc., 225 Park Avenue South, New York,
New York 10003 and represented in Canada by the Canadian MANDA
Group.
CROWN is a trademark of Crown Publishers, Inc.
Manufactured in Japan
Library of Congress Cataloging-in-Publication Data
Euvremer, Teryl. After dark / by Teryl Euvremer.
    Summary: Animals of all shapes and sizes prepare for bed, as described in a
rhyming text.
    [1. Bedtime—Fiction.   2. Animals—Fiction.   3. Stories in rhyme.]
I. Title.
PZ8.3.E898Af   1989   88-14628   [E]—dc19

ISBN 0-517-57104-8

10 9 8 7 6 5 4 3 2 1

First Edition

To Yves

Every evening,
Helter-skelter,
Animals everywhere
Head for shelter.

Three bears like to dilly-dally,

Watch the sun set in the valley.

Then, in total darkness, stumble

Home to tea and apple crumble.

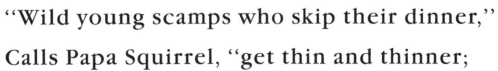

"Wild young scamps who skip their dinner,"

Calls Papa Squirrel, "get thin and thinner;

Shrink till they're the size of ants—

Catastrophe! They lose their pants!

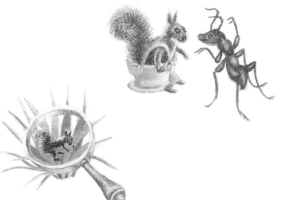

You'd need a magnifying glass

To see them running in the grass.

And then, I fear, they disappear."

Seven foxes, short and tall,
Washing by a waterfall.
Brushing teeth and scrubbing whiskers,
Mother, father, brothers, sisters.

 Portly pigeon, bird-about-town,
In Turkish towel and dressing-gown.

His jabot glows with pearly tints,

His collar's green as peppermints.

From dawn to dusk he does his best

To play the part, to be well-dressed.

But coming from his bath he sloshes

Forth in ankle-high galoshes.

 "You say it's my bedtime?

No siree—

Those pajamas are not for me!

You say it's my bedtime?

No sirrah—

Those pajamas are Hannah's, Ma!"

 Lucky hoppers have the knack,
Like rubber bands,
     of bouncing back.
Too quick to follow with the eye,
Too hard to catch, don't even try!
A tumble, a pounce, a flying leap—
There's more to do in bed than sleep.

Dear rabbit,

    if you've come to dine,

Please make it for another time.

Stop that chomping overhead!

Can't you see we've gone to bed?

A startling story of derring-do
Is told by mother kangaroo,
Of a dashing young squire
Who extinguished a fire
With a bucket of Mulligan stew!

Two animals of different size
Sing their children lullabies,
Play high and low on harp and horn
Until the babes begin to yawn.

Turtle marvels at the moon
Reflected in the deep lagoon.
Very pleasant dreams he wishes
To his gleaming friends, the fishes.

 Plenty of pigs sleep side by side,
Hock to hock and hide to hide.
Mom plants a kiss on each warm snout
Before she puts the lantern out.

How happy is an armadillo
To lay his cheek upon a pillow.
When he can't sleep and wants to talk,
He shares it with his friend, the auk.

 I was nearly asleep
When a monstrous sound
Made me prick up my ears,
Made me leap to the ground.

My fur stood up straighter
Than pile on a carpet.
The house was in darkness;
The front yard was starlit.

And there, cracking walnuts,
Were Papa and Mama!
I let out my breath
And hitched up my pajama....

Some elephants thought
that for a lark
They'd stay up long, long after dark;
Beguiled by the stars till crack of dawn,
They had their breakfast on the lawn.

You snore sometimes,

but I don't care—

I love to feel you sleeping there.

My bed's a little small for two—

But since the other one is you....